To my most favorite people who like to
cha-cha through life with me, thank you!

www.mascotbooks.com

The Paw Paw Fruit Does the Cha-Cha Scoot

For more information, please contact:
Mascot Books
620 Herndon Parkway, Suite 320
Herndon, VA 20170
info@mascotbooks.com

Library of Congress Control Number: 2018900740

CPSIA Code: PRT0218A
ISBN-13: 978-1-68401-530-6

Printed in the United States

THE PAW PAW FRUIT DOES THE CHA-CHA SCOOT

WRITTEN BY KRISSY BYSTROM EMERY
ILLUSTRATED BY JASON HEGLUND

SUITABLE FRUITABLES™
BOOK SERIES

Haven't you heard the latest news?
There's a crazy, dancing fruit on the loose!

Meet Piper the Paw Paw Fruit,
She likes to do the cha-cha...in a suit?!

That slick toe-tapping dance
Will have you stop and stare in a trance.

Moving and grooving her fast and fickle feet,
Sliding and gliding to the sound of the beat.

Green, yellow, and oblong in shape,
You might even see her wearing a cape.

Shhhh! Do you hear that?

Rumba,
rumba

Vroom,
vroom

Is that Piper the Paw Paw Fruit?
Doing the cha-cha...in a suit?

Everyone is trying to spot her in action,
Going incognito is her reaction!

She's a citrus and banana sensation!
Totally leaving you in anticipation.

Boasting her large brown seeds and a creamy texture,
Piper enjoys her baby seedlings doing the cha-cha right alongside her!

Shhhh! Do you hear that?

Rumba,
rumba

Vroom,
vroom

Is that Piper the Paw Paw Fruit?
Doing the cha-cha...in a suit?

She puts on some sunglasses
So no one recognizes her as she passes.

Storing vitamins and minerals inside, she tries to walk normally,
But it's too much—she breaks into the cha-cha informally!

*Zinc (Zn), Vitamin B1 (B1), Magnesium (Mg), Vitamin C (C), Vitamin A (A), Phosphorus (P), Potassium (K).

The crowd is in a frenzy trying to find her,
She grabs her cape and spins into a blur!

In the midst of all this action, she is spotted taking a selfie!
Wanting to remember this moment as she ripens quite quickly
with a short life on the shelfie!

Shhhh! Do you hear that?

Rumba,
rumba

Vroom,
vroom

Is that Piper the Paw Paw Fruit?
Doing the cha-cha...in a suit?

Onlookers rush in to see the commotion,
As she moves down the street in a groovy locomotion.

She quickly snaps a few more selfies to send,
For her time undercover is limited and she needs her friends.

She hopes they can help her out
So she won't have to endure a cha-cha drought!

Shhhh! Do you hear that?

Rumba,
rumba

Vroom,
vroom

Is that Piper the Paw Paw Fruit?
Doing the cha-cha...in a suit?

Her friends convene to discuss,
They ask her why she's making such a fuss.

There is no reason to be all hush-hush,
When everyone just wants to join in the cha-cha rush!

Piper pauses to consider, slides down her sunglasses,
And without hesitation joins in with the masses!

With her pals' encouragement to be herself and do her thing,
She quickly busts into the cha-cha swing!

Shhhh! Do you hear that?

Rumba,
rumba

Vroom,
vroom

Piper the Paw Paw Fruit
Is quite clearly doing the cha-cha scoot!

She gives her undercover ways a boot
And now enjoys cha-cha-ing with the group.

Now when you decide to try a Paw Paw,
Don't be surprised if you start to do the cha-cha.

Maybe not in a suit,
But that certainly would be cute!

MORE ABOUT
THE AMAZING PAW PAW

Where do I grow?

I can be found growing in the eastern half of North America, from the snowy north down to the sunny south.

What do I taste like?

I am a delicious citrus-tasting blend of mango-banana-cantaloupe that varies depending on the variety of the paw paw you try. I also have a creamy, textured flesh that can be compared to that of a banana.

What do I look like?

I am an oblong-shaped fruit and typically green in color with brown blotches that appear as I ripen. I can be anywhere from three to six inches long and have large brown seeds. Try me if you can find me.

What is special about me?

I'm a member of the custard apple family which typically grows in warm, tropical climates. I am quite unusual because I can grow almost anywhere, even places where it snows. Grocery stores don't usually sell me because I have a short shelf life and bruise easily. However, you can grow me in your garden, look for me at farmers' markets during my harvest months of mid-August through October, or even go for a walk in the woods to find me, pick me, and put me in your pocket.

Why am I good for you?

I hold loads of nutrition to help you grow big and strong. If you like apples, oranges, or bananas, I have much more to offer. I'm bursting with vitamins and minerals such as Vitamin C, Vitamin A, Vitamin B1, Magnesium (Mg), Potassium (K), Zinc (Zn), Phosphorus (P), and more!

How do you eat me?

You can eat me after I'm freshly picked—just peel, eat, and toss my seeds! Some of the best uses come when I'm used as a purée in recipes for muffins, pudding, ice cream, sorbet, smoothies, or even salsa.

How old am I?

I have been enjoyed for centuries. Native Americans and European settlers devoured me as a delicious treat and used me for medicinal purposes, too. I guess you can say that I am quite old!

SUITABLE
FRUITABLES™
BOOK SERIES

The original inspiration for Piper the Paw Paw Fruit.
~Owen Emery, age 11